WHISPERS OF ALBION

A JOURNEY OF HOPE

RENAE EDWARDS

CONTENTS

PROLOGUE

SIMON PETER RAN THROUGH the winding streets of Jerusalem, his sandaled feet slapping against the cobblestones. His mind raced as he replayed the scene over and over in his mind. With tear-filled eyes, another wave of panic rose inside him. He needed to find somewhere safe. He had to escape prying eyes and anyone who might recognise him.

The city gates loomed before him, illuminated in the moonlight. Without a second thought, he raced through them and into the quiet countryside beyond. The night air chilled his skin as he stumbled across the meadows, searching for relief from the storm raging inside him.

Exhausted, Peter entered a small garden and sank to the ground. His breath poured out in angry waves as he wiped his tears with trembling hands. In the stillness, soft whisperings of peace battled against the shame and regret threatening to pull him into a dark abyss.

As dawn broke over Jerusalem, Peter's tears continued to fall. How could he have been so foolish? Why had he been so weak? Frustration mixed with disgust as he reflected on his actions. As the image of his Master's face filled his mind, the memories of his failure pelted him like a heavy rain.

CHAPTER ONE

WHISPERS OF WARNING

E *ARLIER THAT NIGHT...*

In the fading twilight, a small group of men travelled the dirt paths just beyond the streets of Jerusalem. Simon Peter, known for his boldness, strolled beside Jesus. The group had just left the Last Supper, and their hearts were burdened by the memory of what their Master had told them. He had spoken of betrayal. Could one of the twelve who had followed and served with Jesus turn him over to the enemy? The Master seemed to think so. A sense of dread caused Peter's stomach to churn.

As they continued their journey, Jesus' voice interrupted the silence. "All ye shall be offended because of me this night: for it is written, I will smite the shepherd, and the sheep shall be scattered. But after that I am risen, I will go before you into Galilee."

Peter's heart raced, his steps faltering. Did he hear that right? Surely, Jesus didn't mean they would all forsake him. Peter squared his shoulders and held his head high. He couldn't speak for the others, but he knew where his devotion and loyalty lay. Nothing could cause him to betray his Lord. Of that, he was sure. His voice echoed off the trees, "Although all shall be offended, yet will not I."

The other disciples exchanged glances while Jesus' gaze rested on Peter. He knew what was in the disciple's heart. He was aware of the hunger that burned within him and the sincerity of his pledge. Peter meant well, but the sad truth was he had no idea what was about to take place. But Jesus knew, and as much as it pained him, he had to prepare his impulsive follower for the upheaval ahead.

"Simon, Simon, behold, Satan hath desired to have you, that he may sift you as wheat: But I have prayed for thee, that thy faith fail not: and when thou art converted, strengthen thy brethren."

Stubbornly, Peter clenched his jaw and felt the heat rising from his neck to his cheeks. He gritted his teeth against the rebuke and shouted with an arrogant cry, "Lord, I am ready to go with thee, both into prison, and to death."

A look of sadness flickered across Jesus' eyes. "Verily I say unto thee, That this day, even in this night, before the cock crow twice, thou shalt deny me thrice."

Peter swung around and looked his Master in the face. His heartbeat pounded in his ears as he clenched and unclenched his fists in irritation. "If I should die with thee, I will not deny thee in any wise."

"Nor I," chimed in Andrew.

"Me neither," added John.

The others murmured in agreement as they continued on their way. Moonlight illuminated the trail, casting eerie shadows that mirrored the group's mood. The only sound was the crunch of their feet against the stony ground.

Before long, the Garden of Gethsemane came into view. Though Jesus' rebuke had wounded his pride, Peter knew he was willing to die for his Master. He had witnessed the miracles of the Messiah and the compassion in his eyes. He had shared in moments of profound teaching and had become part of a brotherhood bound by a common goal. He had left his job, family, and everything he owned to follow this man he believed to be the Son of God. He loved him more than life itself, and if given a chance to prove that, he would gladly do so. His brooding was interrupted by a shaky voice.

"Sit ye here, while I shall pray," Jesus commanded, pointing to a place where several large stones jutted from the ground. The disciples settled onto their makeshift seats of rock and moss while Jesus retreated into the shadows to pray.

As the darkness settled in, the disciples whispered among themselves. James' voice grew louder as he asked the question shared by several in the group. "Anyone else notice Jesus seems off tonight? He's got this sadness about him."

John shifted, looking thoughtful. "Yeah, it's like he's carrying the world on his shoulders."

Tension filled the air as Peter chimed in. "With all this talk of betrayals and denials, is it any wonder? Besides, the religious leaders have been looking for ways to stop him for months, and we've been on the move without a break for more days than I can count. He's probably just worn out like the rest of us. He has a right to be on edge. Let's give him some space. I'm sure he'll be back to his old self tomorrow."

Minutes passed, and the conversation waned. One by one, the disciples succumbed to exhaustion, only to be awakened a short while later by Jesus. "Peter, Simon, sleepest thou? couldest not thou watch one hour? Watch ye and pray, lest ye enter into temptation. The spirit truly is ready, but the flesh is weak."

Once again, Peter's face reddened, embarrassed by another rebuke from his Master and friend. He wasn't the only one who had fallen asleep. Why did Jesus feel the need to single him out? After waking the rest of the group, the sullen disciple stood and began pacing to clear the fog from his head and cool his rising temper.

Jesus returned to his place of prayer as Peter turned away and gazed into the fire. After wetting his dry throat with water from his water-skin, he dropped to his knees on the cool earth, determined to follow the instructions of his Master. The sand shifted beneath him as he prayed, and he repositioned himself to get more comfortable. The low hum of insects and the wind in the trees blended in a soothing melody.

Peter awoke to find Jesus standing beside him. Though his expression was compassionate, his words of disappointment carried a sting. Peter berated himself for his weakness. He hadn't intended to fall asleep, but he was so tired. Jumping to his feet, he stoked the fire and paced the surrounding area, hoping the cool night air would relieve the fatigue. Once he felt more awake, he returned to his knees. With his eyes closed, he furrowed his brow in concentration. He prayed out loud to help clear his mind and keep himself alert. Yet, as weariness overcame him, he drifted to sleep again.

At the sound of Jesus' voice, Peter's heart skipped a beat. He looked into his Master's face, and the sorrow he saw there was unmistakable. But there was something more that caused the disciple to study Jesus closely. His face was wet. It could have been tears or maybe sweat, but there was something else. *Is that blood?*

Refocusing his attention, Peter listened as Jesus warned them of the impending danger. "Sleep on now, and take your rest: it is enough, the hour is come; behold, the Son of man is betrayed into the hands of sinners. Rise up, let us go; lo, he that betrayeth me is at hand."

Chapter Two

Clash of Steel

B efore anyone could understand what Jesus was saying, the sound of hurried footsteps shattered the garden's stillness. Judas Iscariot, who had once been counted among Jesus' closest followers, emerged from the darkness. His face was twisted with betrayal and anguish as he approached the clearing, trailed by an angry mob brandishing swords, spears, and torches.

The former disciple kissed Jesus on the cheek, a pre-arranged sign identifying the one who called himself Lord. The Messiah stared at his betrayer with a mix of sadness and understanding. In turning his back on Jesus, Judas had sealed his own fate. Jesus mourned as much for that as he did for the suffering he knew he was about to endure.

Peter looked on as Jesus calmly conversed with the multitude before them. Confusion and anger coursed through him as he realised the magnitude of the situation. This what was Jesus had been trying to tell them. This was the very thing he had foretold. At this moment, the Messiah was being handed over to those who sought to silence him permanently.

Peter's heart thundered within his chest as his eyes darted between Jesus and the approaching mob. Endless rows of people gathered, gesturing with their torches as their angry cries reverberated in the disciple's ears. His fingers curled instinctively around the hilt of his sword, the cold metal comforting against his palm. In the shadows, he could make out the glint of the enemies' weapons.

The air was tense as the mob closed in, and the events of the evening seemed to move in slow motion. In fear and anger, Peter yanked his sword free from its sheath. The blade gleamed silver in the moonlight as he lunged forward. The clash of steel against flesh filled the air.

The man before Peter cried out in pain and clutched the side of his head as blood poured between his fingers. With wide eyes, Peter looked down to see the man's ear lying on the ground. Jesus' voice cut through the chaos. "Put up again thy sword into his place: for all they that take the sword shall perish with the sword. Thinkest thou that I cannot now pray to my Father, and he shall presently give me more than twelve legions of angels? But how then shall the scripture be fulfilled, that thus it must be?"

Peter's breath was ragged as he lowered his sword. The weight of Jesus' words settled upon him, reminding him that their path was one of sacrifice, not violence. As the truth of his teacher's many lessons echoed in his mind, he felt his grip loosen. With his head bowed, he quickly resheathed his weapon and stepped back into the shadows.

Jesus moved forward and picked up the bloody ear from the ground. He beckoned the injured man closer and placed the ear against the side of his head. Miraculously, the blood vanished, leaving the man wholly restored. It was as if the destructive blow had never happened, leaving the man without a mark or scar.

After a moment of shock, the mob closed in further. Despite what they had just witnessed, their cruel intentions were clear. They wanted Jesus, no matter the cost. And so, obeying his Father's will, the Messiah willingly surrendered himself. The scene unfolded in a blur—Jesus' calm acceptance, the disciples' bewildered expressions, and the mob's triumphant arrogance. As they led Jesus away, Peter's eyes never left his teacher's form.

The mob's torches illuminated the path. Peter's chest tightened as he followed the crowd from a distance. His heart was heavy with what had happened, and the screams of battle echoed through his mind. He had tried to protect Jesus, but instead of staying loyal to what his teacher had exemplified, he resorted to violence and chaos. He had lashed out, forsaking everything Jesus had taught him.

But though he had made a mistake, his determination pulsed through him. He would make things right. He wouldn't make the same mistake again. He would not forsake his friend in this hour of need. He would remain by his side and fight for him the right way. This time, he wouldn't fail.

CHAPTER THREE

TRIAL BY FIRELIGHT

HE NIGHT SETTLED AROUND Jerusalem like a heavy curtain, casting a veil of darkness over the city. As chaos swirled within its walls, Peter stood at the edge of a courtyard. The crackling flames reflected the turmoil that roared within his heart.

The trial of Jesus was underway within the courtyard walls as rumours and whispers echoed in the night air. Peter stood with his back to the wall, his arms folded across his chest, as he watched the confusion around him—a blur of faces telling a story his heart didn't wish to hear. He was no longer within the inner circle, walking beside Jesus. He was a stranger in this group. Peter felt the hair on his neck bristling with apprehension as the throng of onlookers crowded around the courtyard.

Cautiously, a woman approached, her gaze fixed on him. "Thou also wast with Jesus of Galilee," she said, her voice cutting through the tense atmosphere. Her eyes held curiosity and suspicion, and she waited silently for an answer.

A knot formed in Peter's stomach. The memory of his bold proclamation earlier that evening loomed large, and yet, faced with the reality of the situation, his courage wavered. His tongue felt heavy with uncertainty.

"I know not what thou sayest," Peter replied, his voice laced with nervousness. He was like a fish out of water; being a lifelong fisherman, he knew exactly what that looked like. He tried to calm his nerves and steady his knees as his denial reverberated through his mind. And then he heard it. In the distance, a cock crowed. Its mournful call played in Peter's mind like a haunting melody.

As the minutes ticked by, the fire's glow illuminated the courtyard, making it more difficult for Peter to blend into the shadows. Noticing the looks of suspicion cast his way, he pulled the hood of his cloak over his head, hoping to hide his identity. Despite the warmth of the flames, the disciple shivered. Before he could stop the trembling in his body, another figure approached. "This man was also with Jesus of Nazareth." His words echoed off the courthouse walls.

Suddenly, the air tasted like ash and death. Peter glanced around, his palms growing clammy as the eyes of those around him seemed to narrow in scrutiny. He was a disciple, a follower of the one they were accusing, and the tension was nearly more than he could bear. He instinctively gripped the hilt of his sword, but as the memories swept over him, he released his grip. *This is not the way,* he reminded himself.

In desperation, Peter snapped at the man, hoping the people would take the hint and leave him alone. "I know not the man!" he spat. His heart sank like a stone. A chill ran down his spine as his words pierced the night air. He was no longer just a witness to this trial but also a participant. He felt his face flush with guilt and shame as he stared back at his accuser. Peter's mind raced again with memories of that evening in the garden. He had boldly proclaimed his loyalty, only to follow it with his cowardice when Jesus was arrested. And now here he was again, his actions denying what was in his heart. What was wrong with him?

His body tensed as fear surged within him. For the first time in his life, Peter felt lost and alone. But then, he remembered the comforting promise Jesus had made to his disciples that they would never be forsaken or alone. The Savior had assured them that he would always be with them. The memory brought a smile to Peter's lips, but it was short-lived.

Another voice cut through the night like a knife. "Surely thou also art one of them, for thy speech bewrayeth thee."

At this allegation, several men and women turned to stare at him. Peter's heart raced, his breathing shallow and erratic. He had been recognised despite his disguise and attempts to hide in the shadows. This time, his speech was the betrayer. The disciple's heart warred within him. The weight of his promise to Jesus increased with every beat of his heart. As the turmoil raged within him, he wrestled with whether to keep his word or turn away from all he had ever known. His life was on the line here, but hadn't he said he would die for Jesus?

Peter's chest tightened as he cursed, his eyes brimming with tears. With each syllable, he felt something inside him shatter, and as the sound of a distant cock crowing pierced the air, he knew there was no turning back now. Ashamed, Peter looked around to see if anyone he knew had witnessed his utter failure, and immediately, he locked eyes with Jesus as he was being led from the courthouse.

Their silent exchange spoke volumes. The weight of their history, the depth of their relationship, and the significance of Peter's denials hung like a dark cloud between them. And as the cock's crow echoed in the disciple's mind, a wave of despair crashed over him, leaving him breathless and shattered.

Peter stared in horror before turning on his heels and sprinting away from the scene. His legs felt like lead, and his heart was heavy with an unbearable sorrow that threatened to collapse him. As he ran, he gasped for air. Tears of anguish blurred his vision as he stumbled along, giving no thought to where he was headed. The night seemed to swallow him as he wandered in search of escape from the man he had become.

The cock's crow had marked not just the passing of time but also the passing of a moment that would forever be etched in Peter's memory. The moment he had failed the Man he loved most.

CHAPTER FOUR

DAWN OF REGRET

*B*ACK TO WHERE OUR *story began...*
As the sun continued its ascent, it did little to warm Peter against the cold emptiness that overshadowed him. His gaze fell upon his sword—the one he had wielded in the heat of the moment. It lay on the ground beside him, a silent witness to his recklessness.

Peter gripped the hilt. He stood, his gaze fixed on the blade and his heart a tempest of roiling emotions. He had let fear, doubt, and weakness rule him, and his resolve had shattered like a clay vessel.

With a surge of frustration, he thrust the sword downward, intending to bury it in the soil. The blade struck with a dull thud. Confused, he studied the weapon further and realised the sword had not struck soil but stone instead. Even the ground seemed against him on this bleak night as the weapon stood lodged in an unyielding rock.

Desperation surged, compelling him to free the sword from the stone's grip. He pulled and tugged, straining against the stone's resistance, his muscles taut with the effort. Yet, the blade remained steadfast, its connection to the solid rock unbroken.

The cruel twist of irony did not escape Peter's attention. The sword, once a symbol of his strength, now epitomised his helplessness. Just as he couldn't extract it from the stone, he couldn't undo his mistakes or escape the repercussions of his denials.

Exhausted and defeated, Peter sank to his knees, his fingers tracing the cold metal of the blade. He finally allowed his tears to flow freely after holding them back for far too long. His weeping left him feeling hollow, stripped of his bravado and certainty. After what he had done, Peter had no doubt he was now like the discarded sword—imprisoned and useless.

Time seemed to stretch as he sat there, lost in his thoughts and regrets. Suddenly, a gentle breeze drifted through the garden, carrying the morning light. The smell of flowers and pollen filled the air as the birds began their morning melodies. Startled from his reverie, Peter looked up to see the glow of the early morning sun filtering through the leaves in the garden and giving his surroundings a heavenly appearance. The beauty filled him with a newfound awareness, and despite his sorrows, a tiny spark of hope stirred within him.

Peter rose to his feet and returned to where he had left his sword embedded in the stone. He glanced at it before turning away and continuing his journey. He knew he would carry this experience with him always. It would be an ever-present reminder that strength doesn't come from power or weapons. It doesn't come from within oneself because while the spirit is often willing, the flesh is weak. No, strength comes from total dependence on Christ and Christ alone.

With each step forward into uncertainty, Peter determined to face life head-on with courage and resilience no matter what lay beyond the horizon. He would put his trust in Christ and not in himself. He knew now that he could not be trusted, but God was always faithful. Though the weight of his shortcomings pressed upon him, he walked on, hoping that somehow, at some point, he would find a way to make things right.

CHAPTER FIVE

BURDEN OF SILENCE

A MID THE NOISE AND confusion of Calvary's hill, Joseph of Arimathea witnessed the unfolding tragedy. The sky was a swirling mix of grey and black where ominous clouds had gathered and blocked out the sun. The branches of the surrounding trees danced and swayed as if trying to protect themselves from an oncoming storm. Joseph felt the tension and dread that seemed prevalent in the crowd. A shiver ran through him as the light continued to fade, leaving behind only silhouettes and shadows.

Around him, the cries of anguish and despair mingled with the jeers of the onlookers. The air was heavy with the metallic scent of bloodshed. It felt alive, pulsing and throbbing like a living, breathing thing. Joseph's chest tightened. Despite the gory scene before him, he couldn't shift his gaze from the figure hanging on the middle cross.

Haunted by the memory of Jesus being led away by the furious mob, Joseph's heart ached with the knowledge that he had stood on the sidelines. Somehow, in the beautiful Garden of Gethsemane, he had allowed fear to hold him back from defending the man he had come to admire.

In addition to the swirl of emotions within him, there was an overwhelming sense of guilt. He had been a secret follower of Jesus, admiring his teachings and marvelling at his compassion. Yet, when the opportunity arose to stand with him and prevent the unjust arrest, he hesitated. He was held back by his ties to the very religious leaders who sought Jesus' downfall. Friends who held positions of power in the Jewish council. Men he had known for years. Their disapproving glances had silenced him. His courage had faltered, and his regret for that moment of weakness threatened to suffocate him.

And now, Jesus was at the very centre of this cruel spectacle. The sight was heart-wrenching. He was bruised and battered. His body bore the marks of a brutal scourging, and the sounds of pain echoed in his laboured breaths. The earth seemed to roar in agony, and the force from the ground shook everyone. People tumbled and fell while a new wave of dread spread throughout the crowd. Those who had remained standing stumbled along as the earth shuddered and quaked.

When the ground ceased its frenzy, Joseph struggled to his feet and looked again at the centre cross. The cries of the condemned men and the jeers of the onlookers rang out from the hill. Others wept openly. Their sobs rang forth as a testament to their grief and fear. The environment was a battlefield of emotions, a collision of the faithful and the scornful.

In stark contrast to the turmoil that swirled around him, Jesus remained remarkably still. His eyes of love met Joseph's gaze for a fleeting moment. In that exchange, a flow of understanding passed between them.

And then, amid the unrest, a cry shattered the air—an exclamation that rang out with triumphant finality. "It is finished!" Jesus had spoken, and as the words left his lips, his head dropped forward in death. The words, though spoken with weariness, resonated with a profound power. They carried the weight of a life of purpose and a sacrifice willingly given. As the declaration echoed through the crowd, a hush fell over the hill. The darkened sky seemed to hold its breath as if all creation paused to witness the moment.

Joseph's hands trembled as he considered the consequences of his inaction. The trial, the mockery, and now the crucifixion. He ached with regret, knowing if he had found the courage to speak out and oppose the unjust trial, he might have saved his beloved teacher from this death sentence. The cold silence of the crowd felt like a crushing weight on his chest. His heart sank as he looked up and saw Jesus with his eyes closed in death. The gruesome scene spoke crushing words to his heart—"Too late!"

As he looked on, his tears mingled with those of the countless others who had gathered to witness this moment. He felt a deep sense of sorrow but also a strange undercurrent of hope. The cross—a symbol of suffering and sacrifice—somehow became an emblem of victory. Though Joseph didn't fully understand the source of this new hope, he couldn't help but believe that this wasn't the end of Jesus' ministry. Somehow, his teachings would live on, and countless lives would be changed.

Joseph knew he couldn't change the past, but he could take action now and perhaps even impact the future. His thoughts turned to his tomb—a tomb hewn out of rock, a place of rest for his family. The idea formed in his mind of a gesture of respect and honour for the man he had failed to protect. Determined, Joseph stepped forward, leaving behind his guilt and taking his first step toward redemption. His purpose was clear. He would offer his tomb to Jesus.

Joseph entered Pilate's palace with the resolve of a man on a mission. As he walked up the stairs to the dais, he glanced around at the familiar faces. He couldn't ignore the whispers of accusation, even though he had yet to reveal his true loyalty to Jesus. He swallowed hard, hoping to rid his throat of the sudden dryness that had lodged there. The heavy aroma of perfume and other spices filled the air, and while typically familiar and exotic, they were sickening to Joseph at this moment.

The man from Arimathea, aware of the many gazes upon him, humbly bowed before the governor. The gravity of his impending request weighed heavy on his shoulders. This moment could alter the course of his life irreversibly. If he took this step, there would be no turning back and no more shadows to hide in. The truth of his allegiance to Jesus would be laid bare for all to see. He hesitated, contemplating the potential consequences that loomed before him. Could he genuinely risk it all—his esteemed position, his accumulated wealth, perhaps even his life and the safety of his family?

"What is it?" Pilate's voice cut through the tension, forcing Joseph's gaze to meet the magistrate's eyes.

Joseph held the gaze with a steadying breath, his voice clear and unwavering. "With your permission, I would like to bury the body of Jesus in my family's tomb."

Pilate's arched eyebrow indicated his curiosity. "Indeed? And why is that? Is he a relative?"

A lump formed in Joseph's throat, and sweat dampened his brow. There was no room for indecision, no more place for secrecy. It was time to take a stand. Gathering his resolve, he raised his voice, letting his words resonate through the crowd. "No, he is not family, but he was my friend."

Amid the murmurs and shifting gazes that rippled through the assembly, Joseph's words rang through the air, a declaration of loyalty to the man whose lifeless form hung on the cross. The Jewish leaders quickly protested and hurled accusations and assumptions about

Joseph's motives. Yet, despite the storm of opposition that encircled him, Joseph stood steadfast.

As Pilate deliberated, his wife stepped forward, her words in hushed tones meant only for his ears. Joseph observed the exchange, a flicker of curiosity dancing in his eyes as he awaited the governor's response. Pilate's eyes closed, his fingers absently grazing his beard as he weighed the implications of the request. Finally, he broke the silence, his voice firm yet measured. "Very well. However, you must oversee the removal of the body from the cross and make all necessary arrangements for its transfer to the tomb. My resources are stretched thin, and I cannot afford to allocate men for such a task."

Turning away from the magistrate, Joseph licked his chapped lips in relief. The moment had arrived to carry out the act he had set in motion and honour the man who had touched his life and the lives of so many others. With every eye upon him, he left the palace.

The rustle of robes and the hollow thuds of sandalled feet alerted Joseph to the fact he was being followed. He spun around, squinting into the darkness to make out the figure behind him. After all that had transpired the past few days, he was expecting an enemy. Instead, he found a man of similar stature and age standing meekly before him. The man kept his head low, his hands clasped in front of him. He wore a lavishly embroidered robe with frayed edges and costly sandals caked in dust. His clothing told the story of a man who was once wealthy but had come upon hard times, causing Joseph to wonder if this was a glimpse of his future.

The stranger spoke, disrupting Joseph's musings. His voice was heavy with regret. "Jesus was my friend, too," he said softly. "My name is Nicodemus. I was too afraid to show my face until now. I didn't have the courage to come forward and tell others that Jesus was my friend, but seeing what you did just now at Pilate's hall, I realised it was time for me to stop hiding. Would you please allow me to help prepare His body for burial? After all He's done for me, it's the least I can do."

A wave of compassion washed over Joseph, and he nodded silently in agreement. Together, they approached the cross, their steps measured and movements deliberate. With their heads bowed, the two men carefully removed the body from the cross. The depth of silence in the air was inescapable. As they laid the body gently on the ground, women with tear-stained faces approached and began to anoint it with fragrant oils. With every movement, their hands were gentle and respectful, a testimony to the fact that they considered Jesus a beloved friend.

The fabric used for wrapping was an expensive fine linen made by experienced artisans. Every fold seemed to carry secrets and memories of Jesus' time amongst them, and as they worked, a strange sense of peace descended upon them.

With the task completed, Joseph, Nicodemus, and the small group stepped back, their gazes lingering on the figure before them. The air was charged with a sense of transition, a moment that marked the end of one chapter and the beginning of another.

Together, they carried the body to the tomb—Joseph's tomb. The interior of the rock-hewn chamber felt cool and still, the air heavy with the scent of burial spices. Their conversation remained minimal, as no words could convey their innermost thoughts and emotions as they laid Jesus' body down on the hard slab. The reality of the moment lingered among them.

As the moments passed, the crowd slowly dispersed until all that remained were Joseph and Nicodemus. Though neither man said a word, it was evident from their expressions that they struggled to find the strength to leave the side of the friend they had loved yet failed. And then, as they sealed the tomb, the finality of it all settled upon them. As the men rolled the rock in place, the rumble of stone on stone was enough to drown out Joseph's pounding heart.

He studied his surroundings. The landscape was dominated by rocky terrain with a scattering of scrubby vegetation and olive trees. The low sun cast a glow over everything, and the air carried the aroma of myrrh, cassia, and other burial spices even though the tomb was tightly sealed. As he turned back to the stone now concealing the tomb's entrance, a cold sweat ran down his spine. Joseph's tongue felt thick in his mouth, his throat tight. He wondered if it was the taste of the spices or the moment that choked him. Turning his back to Nicodemus, he whispered a silent prayer of forgiveness.

Chapter Six

Echoes of Agony

A N EERIE STILLNESS ENVELOPED the night as Joseph of Arimathea made his way through the quiet streets of Jerusalem. His heart was burdened, and the weight of recent events pressed upon him like a leaden cloak. The image of Jesus' lifeless body, wrapped in linen and placed within the tomb, lingered in his mind as a haunting reminder of the sacrifice that had taken place.

As he walked, his thoughts were a whirlwind of grief, guilt, and loyalty. The evening breeze carried the scent of flowers and the echoes of distant conversations. But despite the many signs of life surrounding him, a sad emptiness clung to Joseph's heart.

As he turned a corner, his eyes fell upon a sword embedded deep within a stone. His heart skipped a beat as recognition flooded over him. He knew this sword. It was the same one that had cut through the night air in the Garden of Gethsemane, slicing off the ear of a servant. Peter's act of aggression had been etched into Joseph's memory, and this sword stood before him as a physical reminder of that moment.

Joseph cautiously approached the sword, its hilt worn and its blade glimmering in the moonlight. His fingers reached for it instinctively, as if he were somehow drawn to it. The memories of that fateful night in the garden filled him with terror and sorrow. The screams. The bloodshed. The fear that had kept him rooted to the ground instead of stepping forward in defence of the Messiah. It was the night that had altered his life irrevocably.

Determination resounded in Joseph's chest as he grasped the sword and pulled at it firmly. It didn't budge. He growled in frustration as he yanked and tugged with every ounce of strength, but the weapon stayed fast in its stone prison. With each failed attempt, his remorse intensified until his breath was shaky and short.

Joseph stepped back, his gaze refusing to leave the sword. Every muscle was tense. Yielding to his defeat, he felt an immense guilt for not being able to undo what had been done.

With a deep ache, he turned away from the stone and the sword trapped within it. He looked out into the night sky and the blanket of stars filling the darkness. The air was cold and thick with moisture, the smell of rain heavy in Joseph's nostrils. As a light mist began to wet his hair and beard, the man of Arimathea walked through the streets of Jerusalem and continued his journey home.

CHAPTER SEVEN

VISION OF HOPE

T HE CITY OF JERUSALEM was steeped in sadness, its roads hushed compared to the usual bustle of activity. Three days had passed since the crucifixion of Jesus, the man who had inspired hope, challenged norms, and stirred hearts. Those who had followed him walked with heads bowed.

But within this veil of sadness, news began to circulate. Eyewitnesses claimed to have seen Jesus risen from the dead. The city was alive with speculation and spirited discussions that swept through its streets like wildfire.

And yet, on the heels of this astonishing gossip came whispered tales of conspiracy. Rumours spread that his disciples had stolen his body and hidden it away so it would appear that he had risen from the dead. The air was thick with suspicion.

The Pharisees and religious leaders huddled together in a shadowy corner. Tension filled the air as news of the disciples' supposed defiance reached them, and they issued arrest orders for those who dared challenge their authority. Outside, crowds hurried through the streets, some in fear of being arrested and others rattled by the political and spiritual unrest.

Joseph stumbled through the dark alleyways, uncertain who to trust. Sweat dripped down his forehead, and his heart thumped wildly as he navigated a seemingly endless maze of danger. He had once been a friend to those who now sought to silence him. They knew where he lived and worked. It was only a matter of time before they found him, and Joseph couldn't help but wonder what would happen then.

That night, as he lay in restless slumber, he had a dream that seemed to bridge the gap between reality and the celestial. In the vision, he stood in a place of light. The brilliance was familiar yet painfully bright; try as he might, Joseph couldn't identify its source. An angelic figure stood before him, leaving him stunned and trembling.

"Joseph of Arimathea," the angel's voice echoed, each word imbued with a weight that vibrated deep within Joseph's soul. "Fear not, for I bring thee tidings of great joy."

Joseph's heart raced as he gazed upon the angel. His thoughts were a blur of conflicting feelings, which had become a common occurrence with him of late. "Who art thou?" he managed to utter.

"I am a messenger of the Most High," the angel replied, his gaze unwavering. "I come to deliver a message of guidance and hope."

As Joseph listened, his body shook with fear and wonder. The angel spoke of the rumours, the accusations, and the growing danger surrounding the disciples. He told of the need for Joseph and his family to leave Jerusalem and embark on a journey that would take him to a distant land where he would find refuge and safety.

"Where should I go?" Joseph asked.

"It is a land far from here, one to which the Most High will guide thee. Travel west across the sea. When you have reached your final destination, the Lord will give you a sign."

The gravity of the situation and a sense of urgency descended heavily on him. Could he and his family leave behind the familiar streets of Jerusalem, the people they had known, and the life they had built? He knew the religious authorities had been searching for Jesus' disciples, and now that his loyalty had been exposed, it was only a matter of time until they came after him. He couldn't see what lay ahead, but he could rely on the angel's reassurance and his faith in God, which had been steadily building inside him. Still, doubt tugged at him.

"Fear not, for the presence of the Lord shall go before thee," the angel declared, his voice resonating with assurance. "Thou shalt carry with thee a token of great power—a sword trapped within a stone. Take it with thee, for it symbolises the strength and protection to guide thee on thy journey."

Joseph's thoughts turned to the sword he had discovered on his way home from Jesus' burial. The sword had once been a symbol of aggression and despair, but according to the angel, it was now imbued with the power of hope and guidance.

"I know the sword of which you speak, for I saw it a few days past," Joseph explained. "But when I tried to remove it from the stone, I could not."

The angel smiled and spoke again. His voice was calm and soothing, like whispers in the middle of the night. "It is not for you to remove the sword. That honour belongs to another, for there will come a day when a great king will rise up. This man is destined to unite the lands in the worship of the one true God. Through his reign, the lands will find peace and a deep, abiding faith in Jesus Christ, the world's Saviour. This king—and he alone—can remove the sword from the stone. You will take the sword in the stone and this token as a reminder of all that has transpired over the past few days."

The angel extended his arm, revealing a goblet carved out of a single piece of wood. Its grain was dark and smooth, reflecting the light from the starry sky like oil on water. Joseph stared in wonder at the intricate carvings etched into its surface and couldn't shake the feeling that he was looking upon something divine.

"This Holy Grail is the cup from which Jesus drank at the last supper with his disciples. Though the cup holds no power, it symbolises the eternal life that can be found through faith in Jesus, the Son of God. May it serve as a reminder that good things can come even in uncertain times. Take it with you and keep it safe until it is needed."

Reaching out, Joseph carefully took the cup from the angel's outstretched hands. His fingers tingled as an unseen power coursed through him. Fearful of dropping such a precious relic, he set it on the bedside table as another question formed in his mind. "What of the disciples?" he asked, his voice concerned. "What of those who believed in him? There are many in danger. Are they also to flee?"

The angel's expression was comforting. "The disciples will be guided, even in the face of adversity," he answered in a deep voice. "They shall continue Jesus' ministry and spread a message that will remain relevant for eternity."

Joseph watched in awe as the angel's wings swept toward him, the downy feathers brushing against his skin. The angel's eyes were pools of wisdom and peace, and his hand was outstretched like an offering. Joseph trembled as something intangible passed between them before the dream faded away. He awoke with a sudden rush of excitement and purpose. As he lay in his bed beside his wife, who still slept soundly, he felt like the angel had breathed fire into his soul and lit a guiding path before him.

As the first light of dawn painted the horizon with hues of gold and pink, Joseph stirred from his bed. His gaze turned to the table, where the wooden cup rested. With hands that trembled ever so slightly, he reached out and grazed its surface once more. He felt renewed, as if he had the strength of a boy half his age. But there was something more. He felt joy rippling up inside of him like waves. Hurriedly, he set the cup back on the table lest it overflowed, drowning him in his merriment. At that moment, Joseph knew his journey was just beginning and that he carried a message and a mission far greater than the uncertainty of the world around him.

CHAPTER EIGHT

ANCHORED IN ADVERSITY

THE WEIGHT OF THE angel's message pressed upon Joseph, urging him to leave his homeland for an undisclosed destination. As he paced back and forth in the modest room, he felt the urgency of their situation, knowing that time was of the essence.

Anna studied her husband's earnest face, his honey-brown eyes sparkling with anticipation. She knew how much this mission meant to him, and although she shared his enthusiasm, doubt niggled at the edges of her thoughts.

"Joseph," she said, her voice low and concerned. Reaching out her slender hand, she lightly touched his arm. The gesture offered both comfort and reassurance. " I know we are pressed for time, but there are many preparations we must make—food, money, shelter... The path we are about to embark on is filled with many risks and uncertainties. It would be wise to plan for any unforeseen circumstances."

"I know, Anna. I've been considering our provisions and the means to finance our journey. We're fortunate to have the ships and the wares we can sell." With that thought in mind, Joseph decided to visit his warehouse after they broke their fast, hoping to get a head start on the preparations.

An eerie tension had settled in the streets since Jesus' crucifixion. Joseph's mind raced as he travelled toward his warehouse that morning. A dark vapour billowed in the distance, staining the clear blue sky. Joseph furrowed his brows, a chill running down his spine as he wondered what could be causing such a commotion.

The clouds of smoke grew thicker as the tin merchant approached the scene. The closer he got, the more terrifying the sight became. The acrid stench of burning wood assaulted his nostrils, sharpening his senses and stirring his heart. He stopped in his tracks, and his eyes widened in disbelief.

Joseph's stomach churned as he moved toward the remains of his warehouse. The heat from the fire scorched his skin, and his eyes stung from the smoke. Flames had engulfed everything they owned. The building had collapsed, leaving little more than a pile of smouldering debris. Joseph leaned down and picked up a scorched wooden plank that lay at the edge of the catastrophe. Tears and smoke clouded his vision momentarily.

Beyond the wall of fire, he saw three dark figures slinking away in a flurry of billowing robes. White-hot rage surged through his veins as he recognised their faces. They were religious leaders, the very ones who claimed to represent justice! His fists clenched as he realised they sought to erase any trace of him and, in so doing, any connection to Jesus.

Joseph shuffled closer to the edge of the warehouse, his footsteps crunching against the rocky ground and wooden ruins. He stopped at the remains of a smaller building, its walls still smoking from the blaze. His chest tightened with sorrow as he surveyed the destruction. His gaze focused on the charred remnants of some of his merchant wares.

The tin goods he had acquired were now reduced to ashes. The weight of their value—both in currency and sentiment—hung heavy in the air, a forcible reminder of the lengths his enemies would go to.

A familiar voice broke through the haze of his thoughts. He turned to see Marcus, a friend and employee, hurrying toward him. The man's face was etched with concern as he approached. His eyes locked onto Joseph's.

"Joseph! I saw the smoke from a distance. I feared the worst," Marcus exclaimed.

Joseph managed a grim nod, his throat tight with emotion. "You weren't mistaken. Our warehouse, our livelihood... It's all gone."

Marcus' gaze grew stormy, and his voice dropped into a low growl. "I overheard rumours in the streets yesterday. They say the religious leaders are determined to wipe out anyone who participated in Jesus' ministry. They've grown ruthless, Joseph."

A shiver ran down Joseph's spine as he processed the gravity of the situation. It wasn't just about him. It was about his family, his children, and their future. The religious leaders' actions were a direct threat to their safety and their journey. What would they do? How could they embark on this trip without the necessary funds to see it through?

Joseph felt his stomach twist as he trudged up the road. Every corner held a new fear, and every shadow caused him to cringe in terror. He glanced over his shoulder constantly, searching for signs of anyone or anything unusual. Nothing seemed amiss, yet he couldn't shake the sensation of being watched. The hairs on the back of his neck stood on end. The once safe and familiar city now felt like a battleground.

The journey home was exhausting, and by the time he arrived, the morning events had taken their toll on him. A heavy weight settled on his shoulders as he walked through the door to Anna's look of expectation. But when she saw his sombre expression, her hope quickly faded, and her eyes filled with dread.

"Joseph, what is it?" Anna asked, her voice trembling as she approached him. She studied his face after catching a whiff of the smoke that clung to his robe and hair. "And what's that smell?"

He sighed, his gaze meeting hers. "The religious leaders, Anna. They've destroyed our warehouse. All our goods, our merchant wares, the means to support our journey... It's all gone."

Anna's eyes widened in disbelief, her hand instinctively covering her mouth. "Destroyed? But why?"

Joseph's lips curled into a bitter smile. "They believe I aided in the disappearance of Jesus' body. They're determined to erase any trace of those connected to Him."

Tears welled in Anna's eyes, her heart aching for her husband, their family, and the injustice of it all. "This is madness, Joseph! To think that doing what's right could end in such devastation."

He reached out to hold her gently, drawing her into an embrace. "We must gather what we have left, what money we can find, and leave before they do more harm," he whispered.

Tears coursed down Anna's cheeks. "But what of our home?"

Joseph's heart melted at seeing his beautiful wife, and he knew how difficult it was for her to leave so much behind. With a choked voice and a shake of his head, he muttered the only words that would come. "I'm sorry, my love."

Anna smiled and leaned her head on his shoulder. The path ahead was uncertain and dangerous, but she knew she was not alone. They had each other.

The corners of Joseph's mouth turned up, his brown eyes alight with an inner fire. "I knew that following the path the Lord has set before us would not be without challenges. But I also believe that

He will provide. We have our faith, family, and the determination to honour the message we've been entrusted with."

Anna nodded again and squeezed his hands. "You're right," she said. "We can't let fear or adversity deter us from this mission. We must place our trust in God's plan."

As they stood hand in hand, the weight of their circumstances felt momentarily lighter. The sound of their children preparing their belongings in the adjoining room reminded them of the unity that bound them as a family.

"We'll find a way," Joseph affirmed, his voice steady and unwavering. "We'll sell what we can, take what remains, and embark on this journey as a family. The ships can still carry our hopes and dreams, even if they carry fewer goods."

Anna's eyes shimmered with determination as she nodded. "And perhaps the challenges we face will strengthen our faith even further."

With an understanding smile, Joseph leaned down and gently kissed her forehead. "That's the spirit, my dear. We'll face whatever comes our way with the unwavering faith that has carried us through. God will be our anchor through this storm."

As the family gathered their belongings and finalised their plans, the urgency of their departure became even more pressing. They couldn't afford to delay longer, not with the religious leaders and their supporters on their heels. Their journey was not just a physical one. It was a journey of faith and discovery. It was a journey that would shape the destiny of generations to come.

Yet, amid the flurry of preparation, a bittersweet sadness lingered. Joseph and Anna exchanged a sad glance, their eyes tracing the familiar corners of their home that had witnessed countless moments of joy, love, and growth. Each room held memories etched into its walls. Memories of raising their children, shared laughter, quiet conversations, and dreams were woven into the very fabric of the space.

As they moved from room to room, gathering their belongings, Joseph's thoughts momentarily drifted to the days when Eli and Miriam were just children, their laughter echoing through the halls. He remembered teaching them life lessons, guiding them through triumphs and challenges, and nurturing their spirits. Anna, too, felt the weight of memories: the first steps taken, the heartfelt conversations, and the warmth of family gatherings.

With tear-filled eyes, Joseph closed the door behind them, the sound echoing with finality. They had chosen the path of faith, compelled by the angel's words and the call of destiny. But as they looked around their home for the final time, they knew they were leaving behind a part of themselves—a piece of their history that would forever remain within those walls.

Chapter Nine

Horizon of Destiny

J oseph's family and a few loyal servants who agreed to accompany them worked together to construct a specially designed cart to carry the stone-encased sword. The carriage was crafted with care, its wheels sturdy, and its construction intended to bear the weight of the heavy stone and its precious cargo. They hastily packed their belongings and supplies aboard several more carts and set off toward Joppa, where Joseph's trade ships were harboured. Since they were located a few days' journey from Jerusalem, the tradesman prayed they were beyond the reach of the religious leaders.

The caravan of horses, carts, and companions wound through the western provinces. With a sense of purpose that resonated deep within him, Joseph patted the cloth-covered grail secured in his saddlebag. The rhythmic clip-clop of hooves and the soft creaking of the carts' wheels created a harmonious rhythm. Riding at the forefront of the small group, Joseph led the way on his horse. Beside him, Anna rode with quiet determination. Their children, Eli and Miriam, followed on horseback, their youthful enthusiasm mingled with a touch of apprehension.

Eli, a young man on the cusp of adulthood, looked ahead with curiosity. His broad shoulders and determined stride hinted at the adventures that lay ahead. He ran his fingers through his thick dark hair as he scanned the horizon excitedly while Miriam kept pace at his side. His young sister sat tall despite her smaller stature. Though four years younger, she had a look of understanding, as if she sensed the importance of their journey without knowing where it would lead.

As the sun cast a warm embrace over the landscape, the family continued their trek into the unknown. Upon reaching the port city of Joppa, the shores of the Great Sea beckoned them. Relief filled them as they boarded one of the three ships carrying them and their belongings across the watery expanse. Joseph's heart swelled with hope as he looked out over the deep blue waters and towards the horizon that promised a new beginning. He thanked God for getting them this far and prayed this journey would take them far beyond the reach of their enemies.

Anna stood beside him, her expression of fear replaced by one of wonder as she witnessed the beauty of the sea for the first time. Eli, meanwhile, could not contain his eagerness and looked on with a mischievous grin. Although Miriam was still uncertain about what lay ahead, she was determined to make the most of this adventure.

Joseph had arranged for them to be accompanied by his most trusted crew members and servants, who had agreed to travel with them in search of a new home. With great optimism, they set sail into the unknown with only their faith and courage to guide them.

The open waters offered a sense of peace and liberation. The wind caressed their faces, carrying the scent of adventure and freedom. The rhythmic sway of the ship beneath their feet was a lullaby of hope, soothing the worries that had plagued them the past few days. Little did they know their troubles had only begun.

Their first port of call was the bustling city of Alexandria in Egypt. As the ship eased into the harbour, the family's anticipation mingled with apprehension. As they disembarked onto the bustling dock, they were greeted by the scent of exotic spices and the noise of foreign tongues. The air was alive with the energy of a city that had seen traders and travellers from all corners of the world.

The narrow alleys were lined with stalls—some for fruits and vegetables and others selling clothing and exotic wares from across the seas. The sound of vendors' cries blended with the soft din of birdsong. After sending off the crew to replenish the supplies, Joseph and Anna guided their children through the bustling marketplace. Miriam's eyes widened as she took in the vibrant colours of rich reds, golds, greens, and purples on display. Eli, ever the cautious one, scanned the crowd with a wary eye.

Joseph had accompanied his crew on many trading voyages and was accustomed to the lively surroundings. Anna, on the other hand, had only known the quiet life in her village. Sensing her nervousness, Joseph threw his arm around her and pulled her close. She smiled at him, feeling the tension ease from her shoulders.

For several hours, the family walked the streets of Alexandria, stopping often to look at the many items on display. Miriam admired an intricate jewellery piece crafted from golden filigree, while a handcrafted wooden puzzle box piqued Eli's curiosity. Though many other wares captured their attention, Joseph reminded his family of a sobering truth.

"We must be careful with our money. We have nothing to sell or trade with our warehouses and goods destroyed. The little funds we have will have to last us the entire journey, and we have no idea how long that might be."

As each member nodded in understanding, a cry pierced the air. "Stop him! That thief stole my money pouch!"

Joseph turned to see a slight figure in a hooded robe zig-zagging his way through the crowd and turning down a narrow alleyway. The man who had been robbed and several others gave chase. Instinctively, Joseph reached down to his belt. Panic shot through his heart as he realised his money bag was gone. He patted both sides of his robe and searched the ground around him.

Noticing his odd behaviour, Anna turned to her husband. "Joseph, what is it? You look as if you've seen a spirit."

"It's gone."

Anna looked back to where the thief had disappeared behind several large buildings. "Yes, I'd say he's long gone."

Joseph shook his head and dragged his hand across his face. "No, not the thief. My money pouch. I think we were robbed, too."

Anna glanced down at Joseph's belt and gasped. Frustration battled with fear for control. "What will we do?"

Sighing, her husband replied. "We'll do what we always do. We'll trust the Lord to provide for us. Thankfully, I didn't bring all my money with me. Most of it is still locked up in our room on the ship. Still, this turn of events will make things more interesting."

With a tightened clutch on their belongings, the family pressed forward, navigating the narrow alleys and market stalls. Anxiety gripped them as they clung to each other, their newfound excitement dimmed by the reality of their insecurity.

As they returned to the safety of their ship, the harbour lights cast long shadows on the water. The events of the day served as a stark reminder that their path was fraught with challenges, both expected and unexpected. The bustling streets of Alexandria had taught them a lesson in vigilance, leaving them acutely aware that their journey was far from secure. And with this warning, they set off again across the sea.

CHAPTER TEN

JOURNEY THROUGH ADVERSITY

A S THEIR SHIP GLIDED into the port of Crete, a sense of cautious hope filled the air. The landscape unfolded through rugged cliffs, golden beaches, and charming villages. The gentle breeze carried the scent of salt and adventure, and the family stepped onto the dock with shaky legs.

Crete welcomed them with open arms. The locals were friendly and hospitable, sharing stories of their island and its rich history. Joseph and Anna watched their children's eyes widen in wonder as they explored the many streets, where vibrant flowers adorned whitewashed buildings and lively markets teemed with colourful goods.

The warmth of the Cretan sun seemed to wash away the shadows of their recent trials, and for a fleeting moment, the family embraced the simple joys of life. They sampled local delicacies, conversed with friendly villagers, and marvelled at the island's natural beauty. It was a relief not to feel like the ground was moving beneath their feet. The stillness was a blessing. Their stop-off in Crete became a sanctuary, a brief interlude of peace amidst the unpredictable currents of their journey.

However, halfway between Crete and their next stop, a sudden shift in the winds signalled the arrival of a storm. The sky, once calm, grew dark. Clouds gathered, casting ominous shapes over the ship. The air grew thick with tension as the gentle breeze transformed into gale-force winds. The storm struck with a violence that defied description. Rain lashed at them like a thousand whips, soaking them to the bone. Thunder roared overhead as lightning illuminated the sky in blinding bursts. Waves towered over the ships like menacing giants, their white crests contrasting with the darkness that enveloped them.

The passengers of each ship clung to the railings and each other. Their knuckles were white from the strain as the vessels pitched and rolled, each jarring impact sending shockwaves through their bodies. Joseph's nerves tingled in his limbs. He had faced trials before, but this battle was different. Everything they had was on these ships. If they lost them, they'd lose it all, possibly even their lives.

Every hour felt like an eternity as they battled the storm's raging winds, the sea tossing their boats like a ragdoll. Salty spray stung their eyes as each gust of wind caused their bodies to tense. The sea rose like a living beast, roaring its fury at them, and the dark, turbulent water surrounding them seemed to stretch on forever. But despite their fear and exhaustion, they clung to faith that this too would pass, just as it had every other time their courage had been tested.

Suddenly, as if the heavens themselves heard their cries, the storm began to relent. The winds gradually weakened, and the waves—while still tumultuous—no longer seemed determined to drag them under. Slowly, the ship's wild dance transformed into a weary waltz.

As the storm's echoes faded, a loud cry of alarm echoed across the churning waves. One of the boats had been battered and was taking on water, slowly sinking into the depths of the sea. Panic erupted into a frenzy as the crew and their families scrambled to save what they could from the doomed ship. In desperation, one of the other vessels latched onto the crippled ship. At the same time, its crew worked tirelessly to secure them together, allowing those in peril to climb aboard and salvage what remained of their possessions. An intense wave of relief and gratitude swept over them as they did a quick headcount, confirming that every life had been spared.

Yet, there was still an overwhelming sadness as Joseph and his group watched helplessly. Their supplies and ship began slipping beneath the horizon until only a silhouette remained. With a bitter splash, it vanished beneath the waves.

CHAPTER ELEVEN

SHELTER IN ACHAIA

As they arrived at their next stop, the port city of Achaia greeted them warmly and provided them with a refuge from the relentless storms threatening their journey. Like the other port cities, the streets were alive with the vibrant energy of merchants, traders, and travellers from far-off lands.

An elderly fisherman watched Joseph as he and the crew secured their ships. "You've faced the wrath of Poseidon himself, I see," the fisherman remarked, pointing to some damage on the ship's hull.

Joseph replied as the man approached, his keen eyes studying both ships. "That we did. We lost an entire ship and some of our cargo. But, by God's grace, every person was saved. I have to admit, it feels good to be on land again. I'm not looking forward to hitting the seas again in a few days."

The fisherman arched an eyebrow. "A few days, you say? Heavy storm season, it is. What you faced was just the first of many. Best to batten down the hatches and wait for calmer seas."

The older man's words carried weight, and Joseph knew his family would do well to heed his advice. They took shelter in a modest inn, which served them well as a temporary lodging. The days stretched into weeks. The ships were moored, their sails furled, as they awaited the end of storm season. Though many of Joseph's thoughts were consumed by gratitude for safety and provision, he also wrestled with the relentless question of whether they were indeed on the right path.

As the family settled into the comfort of the inn's warm hearth, Anna couldn't help but notice the dark shadows under Joseph's eyes. She regarded him with a gentle smile, knowing that the journey had taken its toll on him physically and emotionally. Sensing his unease, she gently inquired, "Joseph, what weighs so heavily on your mind? Is it the storm season that delays our departure?"

Joseph took a moment, his gaze meeting Anna's. "Partly, my love," he began. His voice was soft but filled with an underlying tension. "It's more than that. This journey, these lands we're venturing into... It's the unknown that troubles me."

Anna's brow furrowed with concern as she took his hand in hers. "What do you mean?"

His fingers tightened around hers as he blew out a deep breath. "Anna, I've traded and sailed these waters for years, but this... This is the farthest point I've ever been. None of my ships have ventured beyond this stretch of the trading routes. I do not know what lies ahead or what dangers and challenges we may face."

With a tender smile, Anna leaned closer and kissed his forehead. "Joseph, we may not know what lies ahead, but the Lord does. Whatever challenges may come, we'll face them together, just as we always have. And who knows? Perhaps this uncharted territory holds unexpected blessings for us."

Joseph's lips curved into a grateful smile as he tilted his head to meet Anna's gaze. She was a beacon of faith, and Joseph drew strength from her unwavering love. His chest filled with warmth, and the fear that had begun to creep in dissipated. She was right. Nothing was hidden from God. He knew what awaited them and promised to get them to this new land. Despite the anxiety that threatened to overwhelm him more each day, he would trust God.

During their extended stay, the family and crew kept themselves occupied with various tasks. Anna found peace in exploring the city's markets and making friends with the locals. Meanwhile, Eli and Miriam were as curious as ever, strolling down the bustling streets of Achaia and absorbing its vibrant culture. Joseph divided his time between maintaining the ships and seeking advice and information from the many sailors who had made port to await the storms. He gathered directions on which port cities to sail toward and which ones to avoid and sought to discover everything he could about the sea beyond.

Months passed, and the storm season finally began to wane. As the first hints of calmness returned to the sea, Joseph and Anna stood on the shore, watching the waves grow gentler. The winds whispered promises of a new beginning, another fresh chapter in their journey.

As the family began discussing plans with the crew, Joseph was informed that some of them had chosen to stay behind. These families had decided to make a new beginning in Achaia and to establish homes and roots. Though Joseph was heartbroken to lose such loyal friends, he couldn't blame them for following the Lord's leadership in their lives.

Arrangements were made to accommodate the change in their journey. The smaller crew was divided between the two remaining ships, and the cargo was redistributed to ensure balance and stability. As they prepared to set sail again, the ships' decks were alive with a sense of purpose, tempered by the knowledge that the road ahead was diverging for some of their companions.

Joseph struggled to hold back the tears as he gazed upon the familiar faces who had become both friends and fellow travellers. With a final embrace and a promise to keep each other in their prayers, they bid farewell to those who had chosen a different path.

As the sun bathed the world in a warm embrace, Joseph gazed towards the heavens, seeking a sign of reassurance. As if in response to his unspoken plea, a gentle breeze caressed his face. The sky above remained a vast canvas of blue, unmarred by any miraculous vision, but a sense of calm settled in Joseph's heart.

He turned to Anna, his eyes reflecting his faith. Her smile was radiant. The time on land had done her good. Her face was full and flush again. Her eyes no longer held dark shadows beneath them, and her forehead was free of the creases that had lodged there after months on the sea. While the long period in Achaia had not been planned, Joseph and Anna now recognised it for what it was—a blessing in disguise.

CHAPTER TWELVE

NAVIGATING PERILS

THE SEA WAS CALM, its waters sparkling in the warm midday sun. Fluffy white clouds lazily drifted across the vast expanse of deep blue. For once, all seemed peaceful, as if the sea welcomed their journey with open arms. Even the winds seemed to speak a promise, whispering that their new home was within their grasp.

The ships made good time despite the length of the voyage. As the sailors worked diligently, Joseph could be seen pulling on the rigging or lending an extra pair of hands when needed. The mood aboard the ship was one of hope and expectation, and the passengers all shared a sense of camaraderie in their common goal.

At night, the vast darkness of the sea enveloped them, the stars twinkling overhead like a million tiny fireflies. In the eerie silence of the night, one could only hear the occasional creak of the ship's timbers or the distant call of a bird or whale. For these brief hours, all was peaceful and still, making it easy to forget the hardships they had endured and those that may await them.

As they approached the next port city of Carthage, excitement and curiosity filled the air. The harbour was a hub of activity and commerce. Yet, the language that filled the streets was foreign to their ears, even Joseph's. And the customs of the locals left them feeling like the very things they were—strangers in a distant land. Joseph and Anna exchanged concerned glances, recognising the new challenge before them. How would they navigate the intricacies of communication and culture?

In Carthage, they took the opportunity to replenish their supplies, their interactions with the locals a blend of gestures, expressions, and shared laughter. The unfamiliar surroundings were offset by the warm hospitality they encountered, reminding them that kindness reached far beyond language barriers.

As they set sail again, the sea glistened beneath the sun. The sails were taut and full, billowing in the wind that carried the tang of salty sea air. Waves crested in foam, and the ship was pushed onward. The crew, busy tending to the boat, kept one eye on the horizon and one on the waves. The open sea stretched before them, a canvas of blue meeting the endless sky.

The tin merchant spent his evenings in deep contemplation, seeking a sign. The angel had promised the Lord would guide him, but to what end? They had come so far, but there had been no sign, dream, or vision that they had arrived at the place the Lord had in store for them. Joseph longed for a whisper from above.

One evening, as the sun dipped below the horizon in a blaze of orange and purple, Joseph and Anna stood at the stern of the ship. A sense of quiet urgency settled between them. Joseph's gaze fixed on the distant sky and the expanse of sea that held both promise and peril.

"Anna," he began, his voice laced with a hint of vulnerability, "we've journeyed so far, and through every trial, I've held fast to the belief that the Lord was guiding us. But now I question whether we're still on the right path."

Anna's eyes met his. "Joseph, it's only natural to doubt in times of uncertainty. We've been seeking a sign that confirms our purpose, but perhaps we're looking for it in the wrong places. Our faith is what led us this far, and it will continue to guide us. We must trust that the Lord's plan will unfold in due time."

Joseph nodded. "You're right, Anna. Our journey is one of faith; even when the skies are dark and the seas tumultuous, we must continue to trust."

Their journey led them further west, taking them to the small island of Sardinia. With each passing village, their knowledge and experience of foreign customs grew. The people of Sardinia welcomed them warily at first, with both sides unsure how to communicate in a language that was not theirs. But gradually, through bartered goods and shared laughter, trust began to build between them. Every night, the travellers stayed in a different village. This interlude allowed them to rest after weeks of endless travel and to replenish their supplies.

As the family and their crew set sail from Sardinia, they were well-rested and had high hopes for a pleasant journey, but it was not to be. A sudden fever erupted like a blazing inferno through the ships, claiming countless lives and leaving those who remained trembling in fear. Joseph, Anna, and their children watched in horror as the sickness consumed their beloved servants and friends, taking away those who had become their family. Grief weighed heavily on everyone's heart as they grappled with the dilemma of turning back or forging ahead despite the mounting death toll.

Gathering the crew, Joseph called for a council of sorts. "Friends, we've come so far on this journey and faced challenges that have tested our faith and resilience. But we stand at a crossroads now. Many have fallen ill, and we mourn the loss of those who have passed on to Paradise. The path ahead is uncertain, and it's only natural that we feel fear and doubt. Let us seek the Lord's wisdom and guidance in our decision."

Anna's voice joined his, her eyes reflecting their shared struggles and hopes. "We've sought signs from the Lord, waiting for Him to lead us to the land to which we've been called. But even as we yearn for a clear path, let us not forget the journey itself—the lessons, the growth, and the unbreakable bonds that have formed among us. Whether we turn back or press on, our faith remains our anchor."

The day came when Joseph and Anna decided to sail on despite the looming danger ahead. Fear and uncertainty were written on every face, but none spoke a word of retreat. Instead, they resolved to place their trust in the Lord's guiding hand and resumed their journey.

The first days at sea were difficult. The prolonged illness had weakened the crew, and many were weary with grief. But finally, the fever's grip began to loosen, and all who had fallen ill recovered. Before long, they reached a land where the air was sweet and fragrant.

With hard-earned determination, they bounced from one shore to another, searching for supplies and stories that would sustain them for their remaining time at sea. The people they encountered were sympathetic towards their misfortune, and many offered them free food and lodging. Though they lacked familiarity with each other's language or customs, a certain warmth was shared between them.

Joseph couldn't deny that their journey had been difficult, but he was also amazed at how God had cared for them in their hardships.

As the days melted into weeks, the ship's course carried them toward the boundary that marked the transition from the Great Sea to the vast ocean beyond—the Pillars of Hercules.

As the ships navigated the channel, the sea seemed to narrow, hemmed in by towering cliffs on either side. The Pillars of Hercules stood as majestic sentinels. The waters that had been their companions for so long now merged with the great expanse of the ocean, and a sense of trepidation mingled with awe. From the decks of the ship, Joseph, Anna, and their children gazed upon the passage and the stretches of land on either side. As they exited the passageway, the sea beneath them seemed to stretch infinitely, its depths a canvas of mystery.

CHAPTER THIRTEEN

WINDS OF CHANGE

O NE EVENING, JOSEPH'S WEARIED mind found solace in sleep. An angelic presence, bathed in a soft, radiant light, appeared before him in his dreams. "Joseph of Arimathea," the angel began, "your faith and unwavering dedication have not gone unnoticed. Through trials and storms, you have pressed forward, and your faith shall be rewarded. Fear not, for your journey has been divinely guided."

Joseph's hands trembled as the celestial being glowed before him. He stood frozen in awe, clinging to every word that filled the stillness of the night. The angel's message carried a hint of hope and assurance.

"You have been called to journey north, to Gaul, and from there, westward to an isle known as Britannia," the angel continued. "There, you will find the answers for which your soul seeks. The path may be arduous, and challenges may still arise, but remember this. You walk in the footprints of faith, and your steps are guided by the hand of the Lord God Almighty."

With a sense of wonder, Joseph absorbed the angel's words. The message lingered as the dream faded, infusing his spirit with renewed determination. Joseph wasted no time sharing his vision with his family and crew. For months, they had sought a sign that they were on the right path, and now, at long last, they had an answer.

As the ship sailed into the port of Hispania, a world of vibrant hues and sweet scents greeted them. Music from street performers mingled with the chatter of merchants. As the family strolled down cobblestone streets slick with the morning dew, they inhaled deeply of the air so rich with spices they could almost taste them without touching a single morsel. They spent hours browsing the market stalls filled with silver jewellery, pottery, and delicate silk scarves. They marvelled at the locals who spoke so quickly that the family wondered how anyone could understand them. Eventually, they sought information about their journey up the coast and eagerly stepped back onto their vessel with fresh supplies in hand.

As they set sail once again, the winds carried them to Gaul. One evening, as the family gathered in their cabin, Joseph and Anna discussed their dwindling funds. The trials they had faced on their journey had taken a toll on their resources, and the reality of their situation weighed heavily upon them.

"I worry that our funds are running low," Joseph admitted. "We've only enough to replenish our supplies one last time. After that, it will be gone. I don't know what we'll do or how much farther we must go."

Anna placed a comforting hand on his, their fingers intertwining as if seeking strength from one another. "Perhaps there's a solution we haven't yet considered," she suggested softly. "We could stay here on the ship while we're in Gaul. That would save money on an inn. And, maybe we should stay in this city a bit longer than we expected. We could get work and save our money. If we both work, it shouldn't take long."

Joseph's eyebrows knitted together as he contemplated her words. The idea held a certain practicality. "It's true," he mused, "staying here would offer stability, a chance to rebuild our funds. Yet..." He hesitated, the weight of many unspoken thoughts pressing upon him.

Anna's concern deepened as she sensed his inner struggle. "Yet?" she prompted.

"Yet," Joseph continued, "I can't shake the feeling that we're meant to continue. That our journey is not yet complete. Remember the angel's words, Anna? The calling to journey north to Gaul and then west to Britannia?"

Anna nodded, her expression grim. "I remember. But Joseph, we've faced so much. We're weary, and our family has endured countless trials. How can we be sure?"

The moon's silvery glow lent Joseph's eyes a glimmer of resolve. "We pray. God will guide us. I know He will."

Silence settled between them, the rhythmic lapping of the waves providing a backdrop to their thoughts. And in that stillness, they each offered their silent prayers, seeking guidance and assurance from the One who had brought them this far.

Days passed, and their stay in Gaul became a time of reflection and prayer. Joseph shut the door of their room behind him as he left the moored ship for another walk through the village. The narrow streets were already crowded with people going about their daily business. Joseph nodded to those he passed and smiled at seeing children playing in front of their homes. It was a familiar scene he had seen in many towns on their journey, but it felt different here, like an echo of his past coming back to haunt him. He had uprooted his family and dragged them along on this journey. He wished he had some security to offer them. But with the money running out and no idea how long their journey would last, Joseph didn't know the right decision. He needed answers, and somewhere inside him, he knew where they could be found.

As the morning sun illuminated the sky, Joseph and Anna stood at the beginning of a new day. Their eyes met as an unspoken agreement was made between them. There had been no grand dream or miraculous epiphany this time, just a subtle assurance that had grown within them.

"We go on," Joseph said in an optimistic voice.

A faint smile lit up Anna's face as she nodded her head. "Yes, we must go on."

With the decision made, they boarded their ships again and set sail across the frothy sea. Though their funds were low, their faith was in ample supply, and they had no doubt God would see them through the remainder of their journey. The distant shores of Britannia called out to them as they left Gaul behind.

CHAPTER FOURTEEN

TIDES OF FATE

T HE SUN DIPPED BELOW the horizon, casting a threatening gloom over the sea. A bitter chill crept through the air as if nature sensed the impending danger. The wind kicked up a stinging spray that bit into Joseph's face and coated his clothes with salt. He gripped the ship's wooden wheel with determination. Though standing beside him, Anna's voice couldn't be heard above the crash of waves against the wooden hulls.

As each swell propelled them forward, it threatened to heave them onto the rough rocks that jutted from the water. The sea was unforgiving, a turbulent force that tossed their vessels like leaves caught in a gale. The crew worked tirelessly to keep the ships afloat and prayed they weren't in for another significant storm. Their sweat mingled with the salty spray that drenched their clothes.

Cheers erupted from the deck as the crests of waves gradually revealed a sliver of land. It had been a long and arduous voyage on turbulent waters, but refuge was finally in sight. Little did they know their troubles were far from over. One final battle of courage and faith lay ahead.

Joseph's spine stiffened as three black vessels appeared out of the shadows, their sails billowing like vengeful ghosts. Fear spread through the ship as they closed in. Anna grabbed Joseph's arm, and he looked into her eyes, recognising the terror that mirrored his own.

Within moments, one of the vessels had hijacked their flanking ship while the third bore down on them. Joseph heard Anna's terrified gasp as the vessel drew closer until it finally smashed against their boat, sending wood planks tumbling across the deck.

Joseph's pulse quickened, his knuckles white as he gripped the ship's wheel. The vocal threats from the enemy's boat fueled the urgency in his heart. He feared what would happen if they were boarded. Panic mingled with adrenaline as he barked orders to his crew. "Everyone to the oars! We need to outmanoeuvre them! Row! Row with everything you've got!"

The crew manned their positions with coordinated movements and set out the oars. Even Anna and the children took part in the effort to escape. Before long, they began to pull away from the enemy vessel.

Joseph's fingers danced over the wheel, his eyes scanning the water for any advantage. He strained to keep his fear at bay and focus on the task at hand. But as he glanced over his shoulder, his heart plummeted like a stone.

Two enemy ships were now behind and rapidly closing the gap between them. Cannon fire erupted from one of the vessels, and their balls of flame cut through the air with deadly accuracy. The projectiles struck his other ship, igniting the sails and hulls in a blazing inferno. The anguished cries of the crew pierced the air as they leapt into the churning sea, desperate to escape the engulfing flames.

Joseph's chest tightened, torn between going back for those who had been attacked or maintaining his course in hopes of saving those on board his vessel. As he pondered his decision, more cannon fire rang out, its deadly projectiles landing in the water just to the right of his ship. His hands trembled on the wheel as he exchanged glances with Anna, who had run to his side when she heard the explosion.

Eli's jaw clenched from his place at the oars while he looked behind them at the unfolding tragedy. "Father, they need our help. We can't just abandon them."

Miriam, too, had been an eyewitness to the assault. "We can't go back! We'll be in danger if we do," she sobbed, rowing harder as if to emphasise her point.

The ship rocked as a fresh round of cannon fire exploded near the waterline, sending plumes of spray into the air. The pirates were gaining ground, and Joseph's heart pounded. In a moment of agonising indecision, he wrestled with his options. Could they save those left behind? Was the risk too great?

As if in answer, the pirate ships surged forward, coming up alongside their vessel again. The sparkle of malicious intent in their eyes and the glint of weapons signalled the inevitable. Their pursuers were too close, and there was nowhere left to run. As realisation settled over Joseph, he turned to Anna, his voice laced with sadness.

"We can't save them if we're overwhelmed ourselves," he said. "We have to face what's ahead and protect our family. We'll remember them, but we must keep moving forward."

Anna's gaze held his for a moment. Filled with unspoken understanding, she grabbed his hand and nodded. "We'll honour them with our survival."

With a heavy heart, Joseph nodded back. He turned his attention to the crew, his voice carrying a steely resolve. "Prepare for a fight, but only if we must. Let's show them we won't go down without a struggle."

The pirate ships, their sails stained with dirt and the salt of the sea, closed in. The vessels were adorned with fierce carvings of sea monsters, and their flags were tattered by time and wear. Swords glinted in the sun as rough laughter rose from the decks. Joseph could hear the screams of birds above him as he unsheathed his sword. He would protect his family, no matter the cost.

Joseph stood at the helm, his family gathered tightly around him, watching in horror as the pirates drew alongside them. The salty sea air burned their nostrils as they braced themselves for the struggle for survival against these merciless cutthroats who would stop at nothing to claim what wasn't theirs.

CHAPTER FIFTEEN

PIRATES AND PROVIDENCE

A THUNDEROUS CRASH REVERBERATED through the ship as the pirates' grappling hooks latched onto their vessel. The world seemed to spin as the boat was pulled closer. It was then that Joseph made the heart-wrenching decision. He turned to Eli and Miriam, his voice steady as he whispered instructions. As the pirates closed in, Joseph knew their hope rested in their children's courage and faith in the divine purpose that had guided them this far.

"Get below decks and make your way to the storage hold. Find some empty water barrels and hide inside." Joseph's eyes glistened with unshed tears. "No matter what happens, no matter what you hear, stay hidden. The pirates must not know you're on board."

Reaching inside the pouch at his side, Joseph pulled out the Holy Grail and entrusted it to Eli's care. With an unwavering gaze, he spoke to his son. "Guard this at all costs. Keep it hidden with you inside the barrel."

Eli nodded in understanding, and he and Miriam dashed toward the stairs. As the crew gathered their few weapons, Anna sank back into the shadows and fell to her knees, praying for their safety and protection.

The pirate captain's triumphant cry echoed through the chaos, and within seconds, the pirates descended upon them like vultures. Joseph's heart hammered in his chest as he exchanged desperate glances with Anna and gripped more tightly to his sword.

The pirate captain's black eyes were filled with cruelty. In the moon's dim light, his jagged face looked like it had been carved from wood. The sound of steel on steel rang through the night air and, with it, the cries of distress and death. The battle was swift and merciless, like a wild animal devouring its prey. Swords clashed. Arrows flew. The air was filled with confusion. Joseph and his crew fought valiantly, their determination fueled by the understanding that this was more than a battle for their possessions. It was a battle for their lives. Yet, even as they fought, fear clutched at Joseph's chest, fear that they might not survive to see the land God had prepared for them.

In moments, the pirates had overwhelmed the small crew, leaving a grim scene in their wake. The ship's deck was littered with bodies—both wounded and lifeless. Those who had managed to survive were rounded up and bound together. Joseph and Anna could only watch in helpless horror as the pirates methodically raided their temporary sanctuary, snatching away their meagre belongings.

The pirate captain's last orders echoed through the aftermath of the battle, deepening the despair that had already settled in Joseph's chest. "Gather all the provisions! We've got a journey ahead, and we'll need food and water, won't we, mates?" The captain's gaze shifted to the prisoners, his tone a mix of mockery and twisted courtesy. "But let's not be seen as entirely heartless. Leave them one barrel of water. It won't carry them far, but no one can say we weren't generous."

Cold and callous laughter echoed as the pirates turned toward the ship's galley and storage holds. They moved with a chilling efficiency, their eyes scanning for any signs of treasure to seize. In a blink, they reemerged, carrying barrels of water and other plundered provisions. Joseph and Anna's eyes welled with tears as they watched the barrels—two of which held their precious children—being hauled onto the pirate vessel.

The enemies' cruel taunts filled the air as they made their way to their vessel. As Joseph's crew watched them depart, the pirate captain turned back and addressed them with a mocking bow. "All ye who remain have been warned. We will return if we hear even a peep about what transpired here today." With a smirk, he continued, "Not that you'll likely live long enough to tell anyone."

While the remaining pirates made their exit, Joseph and Anna could only hold onto the small comfort that they had not seen the sword in the stone taken away.

As the pirates' ship receded into the distance, the world seemed to blur around them. Joseph and the remaining crew immediately set to work, tugging at the ropes that bound them together. Through sheer determination, one sailor retrieved his knife and deftly sliced through the cords that held them captive. A haunting silence settled over the ship as the ropes dropped to the deck.

Joseph and Anna rushed below deck, their hearts in their throats as they approached the storage hold. Trembling, they forced open the door and felt along the inner wall for the torch. As soon as Joseph grabbed hold of it, a spark ignited. Flames erupted from the end of the torch, filling the room with light and scorching heat. They could feel the intensity of the fire on their skin as it revealed the room's tale of hope.

Joseph and Anna's hearts raced as they peered at the three looming barrels. From within one of them, a tiny sneeze pierced the silence. Confused, the husband and wife staggered forward and yanked away the lids to reveal two familiar figures crouched inside. Miriam emerged first, and then Eli, his grip on the Grail unwavering.

Overwhelming gratitude hit Joseph and Anna like a tidal wave. Tears spilt from their eyes as they embraced their children. They were alive and unharmed! After several moments of joyful reunion, Joseph pried open the last barrel containing water.

Stepping back, he shook his head in bewilderment. "I don't understand. The pirate captain was adamant that only one barrel of water remained. Why didn't they take your barrels?"

Miriam spoke up, her eyes gleaming with excitement and wonder. "They thought these barrels were empty."

At this declaration, it was Anna's turn to be confused. "But surely they would have checked inside and found you. They would have had to look inside to know whether or not they were empty."

Eli, his voice excited but shaky, explained. "That's the crazy part. They did open our barrels. I thought for sure we would be discovered. But they didn't see us when they pried off the lids and looked inside. It was as if we were invisible, like something or Someone was shielding us from their vision. Once they were satisfied the barrels were empty, they left them to save space and weight on their vessel."

Joseph and Anna exchanged glances. They had put their trust in the Lord, and even though trouble had overtaken them, He had protected them and their children. Thankfulness bubbled up inside Joseph until he thought he might explode, and just when he felt he couldn't become any more overwhelmed, he spotted the sword in the stone where it rested in the corner of the room.

"What about that?" he asked the children, pointing toward the sacred artefact.

Miriam excitedly raised her hand, indicating her desire to tell this part of the story. At her mother's amused nod, she blurted out, "The pirates tried to move it, but it was too heavy. They thought they would be clever and take the sword but couldn't pull it from the stone. They tried. Everyone took a turn, but they couldn't pull it free. So, they gave up, said a few curse words, and left it behind."

After returning to the main deck, Joseph and Anna stared across the sea, clinging tightly to their precious cargo— the two children who had miraculously survived the pirate attack. They whispered prayers of gratitude and thanked God for being faithful to His promise. The scorched air tasted like burning wood and smouldering sails, reminding the family how much they had lost on their journey. A vessel. Dear friends. Everything they owned. Yet they could not help but feel blessed.

As they lay in bed that night, Anna's voice broke the silence surrounding them. "Joseph, are you awake?"

"I am, my love. What is it?"

Anna nestled even closer against his chest. She spoke in hushed tones, mindful not to disturb the children slumbering on the other side of the room. "If we had chosen to stay in Gaul and raise more money, the pirates would have likely taken that, too. Time would have been wasted, as anything we gained would have been lost. Even in that, the Lord was our shield."

A soft smile adorned Joseph's lips, unseen in the darkness. "You're right, my dear. God knows what's best for us, even when we can't make sense of our circumstances."

CHAPTER SIXTEEN

BLOSSOMS OF REVELATION

A FTER A SEEMINGLY ENDLESS journey, the land before them drew nearer, and the inviting countryside beckoned them. As they reflected on the time since the pirate attack, a sense of wonder enveloped Joseph and his family.

They feared how they would survive after the pirates had stolen their food and water. But one morning, they discovered the barrels that had once contained Joseph's children were now filled with grain to bake bread and make porridge.

Despite being consumed daily by all aboard, the water from the remaining barrel never ran dry. Each morning, the keg was filled to the brim. And when they went fishing, more often than not, the nets were so full of fish that some had to be returned to the sea.

Not once did hunger or thirst overcome them during their remaining journey. God provided in ways beyond what they could comprehend, reminding them of His protection and provision even in the darkest moments. Despite facing tempestuous oceans and challenging obstacles, their needs were met.

With a sigh of relief, Joseph and his family stepped off the boat and onto the sandy shores of Brittania. The sand was soft beneath their feet. As they looked around, they were in awe of the beauty of this new land—a land that held the promise of a future yet to be written. The angel's words and the prophecy echoed in Joseph's mind. It was like a symphony of hope harmonising with the waves crashing against the shore.

After taking time to pray and thank the Lord for their safe travels, Joseph—along with his family and crew— embarked, once again, on a journey across an unfamiliar landscape. They set out on the path ahead with horses and a sturdy cart. The days turned into weeks, and each passing mile brought new scenery.

As they travelled through the countryside, Joseph was mesmerised by the lush rolling hills and vibrant valleys. The air was fragrant with wildflowers, and the verdant grass swayed in the light breeze. Sunbeams raced across the sky, bathing everything in an almost magical light.

Yet, beneath the awe, a sense of uncertainty lingered. Joseph knew he was following a divine calling, but the destination remained hidden. The angel had assured him God would send a sign to signal his journey's end, but if there had been a sign, he had missed it.

As the sun cast long shadows across the landscape one evening, the family settled for the night. After tethering the horses, the group set up a makeshift camp. As the stars emerged, Joseph stared at the sky, his thoughts drifting back to all he had left behind, including the comfort of familiarity.

Before lying down to rest, he took his staff—a simple wooden rod he had carried throughout his journey—and thrust it into the earth beside him. It served as a way to anchor himself to this foreign soil and a silent prayer for the Lord to guide him forward.

As the group settled into slumber, Joseph's sleep was restless. In his dreams, he saw a thorned tree unlike anything he had ever seen. Its branches were adorned with delicate white and pink blossoms that reminded Joseph of the crown of thorns placed upon Jesus' head before the crucifixion. The sight was both haunting and strangely comforting.

As he gazed upon the tree, a feeling of reverence enveloped him. He heard whispers in the wind as if the land was speaking to him. And then, the scene shifted, and he saw a familiar figure beside the thorned tree. The angel's voice echoed in Joseph's ears. "Your journey has ended, Joseph," the angel said. "You have arrived at the place the Lord has called you. This is the land of Brittania, though many know it by its truer name, Albion. In the next valley, you will find your new home. Go and teach the people there all you have seen and learned. You carry the most precious gift of all—an invitation of salvation to all who will believe. The Lord will continue to guide you in your quest."

Joseph jolted awake, the dream still fresh in his mind. He shot up from the ground and rubbed the sleep from his eyes, only to be greeted by his vision come to life. The staff he had planted into the earth the previous night had transformed. Its wooden frame had twisted into gnarled thorns that stretched outwards, threateningly sharp. From the branches grew white and pink buds that pulsed like veins. Joseph reached out to touch the tender blossoms but recoiled as a single thorn pierced his skin. It was then he realised this was no mere dream. As he stood there sucking his injured finger, Joseph felt a deep sense of awe and understanding. This tree was a sign that he had reached his destination. They were finally home.

Joseph woke his family with a renewed sense of purpose. He shared with them the dream, the angel's words, and the significance of the thorned tree. After quickly packing up their supplies, the family embarked on the last leg of their journey.

CHAPTER SEVENTEEN

BEYOND EXCALIBUR

THE CITIZENS OF ALBION gladly accepted the newcomers with open-hearted hospitality. Their new home was a land of fertile valleys, rolling hills, and forests that seemed to stretch beyond the horizon. The air was crisp and refreshing, carrying the promise of new beginnings.

Joseph and his family eagerly set out to build their new home. As the family gathered wood, stone, and clay from the surrounding forest, Joseph worked with a skilful hand to craft a sturdy yet elegant structure. Each day, they made progress until the day the walls of the house were finally complete.

When the following morning arrived, Joseph's family opened the door of their home to a brand new world. Joseph's heart was filled with peace and contentment, knowing that this place had been intended for them all along. He thanked God for blessing their journey and vowed to take care of their new home. Albion was not just any place; it was where they would begin their new lives.

Each morning, Joseph and his family joined their new friends, learning the ways of Albion. Together, they planted crops, gathered firewood, and repaired stone fences along the meadows. Although their hands often grew calloused and sore, each evening found them trading stories around a campfire, brewing herbal tea from wild plants, and celebrating their growing connection to this new land.

Once the family was settled, Joseph turned his attention to establishing a place of worship. He dreamed of a sanctuary where the teachings of Jesus could be shared, and the message of hope and faith could take root and grow. While the native people were kind and gracious, their knowledge of God was limited. In their ignorance, some even worshipped idols made of wood, stone, or brass. With a desire to introduce his neighbours to the one true Savior, Joseph led his family, servants, and companions in constructing the first chapel in Albion. They worked side by side, their hands building up the walls that would soon bear witness to their faith.

The chapel was slowly constructed, its four walls and high ceilings a testament to the devotion of the many workers. The scent of cedar drifted in the air as light streamed through the open windows, coating every crevice of the chapel in its divine glow.

The sacred scrolls of Scripture from Jerusalem, which Joseph assumed had been stolen by the pirates, had miraculously appeared in the sanctuary one night and found their place within the chapel's hallowed shelves. Joseph yearned to display the Holy Grail in a position of reverence, yet he held back, fearing that the locals might misconstrue its significance and confuse it with an idol. Hence, the Grail remained discreetly concealed, its profound purpose known only to the angel, it seemed.

As the chapel neared completion, the question of the sword in the stone remained. The Holy Grail remained tucked within a sturdy wooden chest at Joseph's home while the sword rested on the ground just beyond its threshold. One evening, as Joseph sought divine guidance through prayer, the Holy Spirit's gentle whisper led him to the lush woods directly behind the chapel. Amidst the serene beauty, Joseph surveyed his surroundings. The clouds gracefully parted, granting the full moon's radiant glow to cast a shadow that materialised into the form of a cross on the ground. Joseph understood the Lord's clear direction and uttered a silent word of thanks.

With the path made clear to him, Joseph returned to his home. Armed with the Grail and a small spade, he ventured once more into the forest, the haunting imprint of the cross still etched onto the earth before him. After digging a deep cavity, he carefully nestled the Grail within and covered it with soil.

Joseph rallied his neighbours as the early rays of the following morning danced through the trees. Together, they harnessed their strength to shift the formidable weight of the sword in the stone into the forest, positioning it above the concealed Grail. The blade gleamed in the radiant morning light—a silent symbol of strength, destiny, and the unity yet to come.

Upon the chapel's completion, a solemn ceremony marked its inauguration. Joseph stood before those who had journeyed with him and the growing community of Albion that had welcomed them. His voice was steady as he recounted the journey that had led them to this land, the challenges they had faced, and the unwavering faith that had carried them through.

As he spoke, he told of the night long ago when he had found the sword in the stone and the angel who had appeared to him a few nights later. The tale resonated with each heart gathered before him. He spoke of the prophecy and the future king who would one day free the sword and unite the land. That king would bring about a time of peace and sincere faith in the one true God. As he spoke, Joseph's words were recorded in the chapel books, etched into history as a legacy to be passed down through generations.

"This is no ordinary sword," Joseph declared, gesturing toward the imposing stone-encased weapon. "This sword, which I have deemed Excalibur, stands as a symbol of profound sacrifice, a reminder of the cross Jesus bore for our sins. He fulfilled His promise by rising from the grave and conquering death. Just as my Lord emerged victorious, this sword symbolises our persistent hope and the eternal life made possible through Jesus Christ. Its blade will never dull, and its surface will never rust. The one who wields it shall gain the might of a hundred. The sword will be a guiding light in the darkest times. However, let us never forget that our reverence is not for the sword but for the Creator who has gifted us with this loving and powerful symbol. Its presence shall forever remind us of His greatness and the incredible deeds He has done on our behalf."

In the following years, the community thrived under the thread of their shared faith. The chapel's significance grew beyond mere construction. It became a cornerstone of daily life, a sanctuary of refuge, and a beacon of hope. Its walls echoed with fervent prayers, the harmonious hymns of worship, and the earnest exchange of stories that recounted the miracles and wisdom of Jesus Christ.

As the seasons changed and the years rolled by, the tale of Excalibur ingrained itself deeply within the soul of Albion. It was an anecdote shared around hearths, a fable whispered in awe, and a legacy handed down from generation to generation. With each passing decade, the legend's roots grew stronger, intertwining with the culture and identity of Albion itself.

At the age of 90, Joseph of Arimathea, the humble and faithful servant, reached the end of his earthly journey. The community he had nurtured and the established chapel continued to thrive even in his absence. His legacy was celebrated in the lives he had touched, the faith he had fostered, and the hope he had sown.

As the torch of leadership was passed to new hands, the chapel's influence grew. Christianity's embrace widened, and the once-novel faith took root in the hearts of many. Chapels dotted the land, each a testimony to the expanding circle of believers who sought to deepen their understanding of Jesus' teachings and continue the legacy Joseph had begun.

However, amidst the triumph of faith, a subtle transformation unfolded over the years. Just as a gentle breeze erodes the hardest rock over time, the clarity of truth began to wane. The tales of Excalibur persisted, whispered by firesides and recounted in storybooks, but the deeper meaning slowly faded. The prophecy itself became twisted and abbreviated, a crucial fragment omitted. Gone was the reference to the future king who would unite the lands through the unifying power of faith in the one true God. The very heart of the prophecy was edited, leaving a void in the narrative that would go unnoticed by generations to come.

And as the prophecy was diluted, so too were the chapels. The very places where faith had flourished began to close, their congregations dwindling. Shadows crept over the land in the form of ancient pagan practices and fleeting "religions" that enticed hearts away from God and the truth of the Scriptures. Slowly, the radiant tapestry woven by Joseph's devotion started to fray.

Amid the backdrop of fading faith, a few symbols of hope persevered. The thorned tree said to have sprouted from Joseph's staff, thrived despite the changing tides. Unlike other trees, it bore its blossoms not once but twice yearly. In the quiet moments of Jesus' birth and again at his resurrection, the tree burst into delicate bloom, its white and pink flowers a silent proclamation of a story half-remembered. Like the sword in the stone, the tree's significance became a relic of history, cherished but unexplained.

The legendary blade, Excalibur, stood tall and proud, a symbol of promise and destiny. It awaited the moment its true purpose would be unveiled, anticipating the rise of the one who would lead the land back to God—the Once and Future King.

And though the tale of Excalibur remained widely known, a precious secret went with Joseph to his final resting place. The location of the Holy Grail remained locked within his heart. The quiet guardian of a sacred trust, he took the knowledge of its whereabouts to his grave...or so it was believed.

HOPE REBORN: CHAPTER ONE

"ADMIT IT, MERLIN, YOU did it on purpose." Arthur spat the words over his shoulder, his bow and arrows bouncing across his back with his harsh, rapid steps.

"Maybe I did. What of it?"

Arthur's blue eyes narrowed. "Oh, I don't know. I guess it would be nice to bag something while out hunting. Don't you think?"

"You really don't want to know what I think," Merlin muttered under his breath as he ducked under the low-hanging branches of the hemlock tree.

Arthur stopped and swung around to look at his childhood friend. "What was that?"

Merlin, too, halted his hurried pace and stared into the frowning face of Prince Arthur of Camelot, who incidentally didn't know he was the one and only heir to the royal kingdom. Repositioning his pack on his shoulder, he shrugged. "I don't like hunting. That's all."

"It's fun!" Arthur screamed, waving his hands for emphasis. "It's just a little sport. Honestly, Merlin, sometimes you're such a baby!"

Something within Merlin ignited, and his temper nearly got the best of him. "I don't think it's fair. You have weapons, but what do the poor animals have? Nothing, that's what! It's just not right. I think you ought to respect all of God's creatures."

"So you did do it?" Arthur squeaked.

Merlin fidgeted, running his fingers through his wavy, raven-coloured hair and averting his eyes of the same colour. "Did what?"

"You know exactly what I'm talking about. You used your magic to make those rabbits disappear."

Merlin smiled inwardly as he reflected on the vanishing spell he'd used on the prince's prey. It was one of the first spells he had learned from his father, but in his seventeen years, Merlin realised that sometimes simple is better, even though he was capable of much greater things. "Let's just say you won't have those rabbit furs for your new winter coat."

Arthur growled, shook his head in frustration, and continued up the narrow trail through the dense forest, Merlin following in his wake. The path was rocky and rooted, made visible only by the many horses and carriages that took the route as a shortcut between the nearby villages. The early morning sun filtered through the trees, displaying glorious rays in the otherwise gloomy surroundings. Beads of dew dripped off the leaves, occasionally sounding like a gentle rain. The trees stood broad and tall, reaching into the heavens with their thick branches and dark green foliage. Small mushrooms of different shapes and sizes sprouted out of the ground on either side of the winding path.

"Deer!" Arthur shouted as he took off into the heart of the woods, his movements displaying the grace and agility he had learned through years of sport, exercise, and sword work.

"Wait!" Merlin cried, hurrying to catch up and possibly avert Arthur's attempts to kill the deer. But it seemed he didn't need his magical powers after all. After a short jaunt through the woods, the young magician came upon Arthur, standing in the rays of golden sunlight and staring at a giant stone. A magnificent sword like none Merlin had ever seen before protruded from the top of the rock. Its handle shone like the brightest gold, and the blade (at least what could be seen of it) bore some form of inscription. The sword appeared both beautiful and deadly, and Merlin knew at once he was looking upon Excalibur.

"Would you look at that," Arthur remarked, circling the sword in the stone. "The blade is stuck fast in solid stone. I would never think such a thing were possible." Suddenly, Arthur stopped and looked straight at Merlin. "This isn't your doing, is it?"

Merlin shook his head and drew closer to view the marvellous attraction. Though his father had spoken about Excalibur, this was the magician's first opportunity to see it himself. "I assure you, it is not, but I have heard tell of it. It is said that only the rightful king of Camelot can remove the sword from the stone."

"Surely, you jest! There's no way anyone could remove the sword from there. It's impossible."

Merlin squatted down to examine the point at which the sword met the stone. "Improbable? Yes. But impossible? I think not. Since the death of King Uther, many have tried to remove the sword and take their place as the rightful king, so it would seem others also believe it is possible."

Arthur joined Merlin on the ground and stared at the gleaming sword. "Yet, for all those who believe, the sword remains locked within the grip of the stone. The whole thing is probably some grand fairy tale to entertain the local children."

Merlin stood and hefted his pack on his shoulder, rejoicing that Arthur would soon know his secret. For years, he had wanted to tell Arthur what he knew of the prince's true identity, but his father had forbidden it and made Merlin promise never to speak of it until Arthur was of age. Even after his father's death, the young magician kept his promise. But today would mark a new beginning. Today, everything would change.

"Fairy tale? Maybe, or maybe the rightful king hasn't tried to remove the sword yet." With a gleam in his eye, he nudged Arthur. "Perhaps you will be the one to remove it. Why don't you give it a try?"

"Me?" Arthur squeaked as he rose to his feet. "How in the world would the son of a lowly farmer be the heir to the greatest kingdom on earth? I think your magic has made you looney, my friend."

"Just try it," Merlin urged. "What's the harm?"

"For starters, I'll look like an idiot when it doesn't come free."

Merlin looked over his right shoulder and then his left. "There's no one here but me."

"Then you try it."

Convinced that Arthur wouldn't cooperate until he had gotten his way, Merlin stepped up to the massive stone and gripped the sword's handle with both hands. With his feet planted firmly on the rock, the magician heaved upward with all his strength. The sword held fast, giving no indication that it had moved in the slightest. He might as well have been trying to lift the stone itself. Merlin released his grip, wiped his hands down his breeches, and tried again. The result was the same. Caressing his achy fingers, he stepped down and turned to his lifelong friend. "Well, there you go. Your turn."

Arthur squinted at Merlin, then turned and surveyed the rock once again. "Fine," he muttered, stepping up to the giant stone. Just as the magician had done, the young prince dried his hands on his breeches and gripped the hilt of the glimmering sword. After taking a deep breath, Arthur closed his eyes and pulled with all his might.

Merlin stood back in anticipation, awaiting the look on Arthur's face when the sword came free. He studied his friend with a critical eye. Though only sixteen, Arthur stood as tall as most men he knew. His broad shoulders and muscled arms revealed how fit and healthy the prince was despite being raised outside the palace. His short blonde hair, bronze skin, and gleaming smile had captured the attention of more than one maiden in his short life. Yes, he certainly looked the part of a king, but more than that, Merlin knew Arthur possessed the character and qualities of a good king. Yes, he was young and untrained, but Arthur would be a great ruler, and Merlin was determined to help him every step of the way. It wasn't chance that had led the two young men. It was destiny. Merlin was sure of it.

Arthur's body shook from the exertion, but the sword remained steadfast as before. Not a sound of grinding or shifting. Arthur adjusted his stance and his grip on the blade and tried again. Nothing. Merlin felt his jaw drop as his mind began to spin with questions. What was happening? Arthur was the rightful heir to Camelot, even if he didn't know it himself, so he should be able to release the sword. Why wasn't it working?

"See, I told you," Arthur said as he turned and walked away from Excalibur. "No farmer's son is going to rule Camelot."

Merlin surged toward Arthur, pushing him back toward the stone. "Wait! Something's not right. Try it one more time."

"What's the point, Merlin? I don't think even the rightful king could pull that sword free. It's just not possible."

"But, I mean, it should," Merlin stammered, his voice full of desperation. "Please, Just once more. . . for me."

Giving in to his friend's pleas, Arthur stepped up to the stone again and wrapped his fingers tightly around the sword's hilt. As he tugged on the mighty weapon, Merlin began muttering a spell under his breath. It was an enchantment he had never used before, but he was sure if ever there was a time to use it, it was now. His father had assured him it was Merlin's destiny to guide, help, and protect Arthur, but Merlin had never anticipated that the help would begin so soon. Still, if the sword wouldn't come free for Arthur, what choice did Merlin have but to help him out a little? After all, that was the purpose of his magic.

As the young magician reached the end of his spell, a dark cloud formed over the sword and soon grew more extensive than the stone itself. The brilliant rays of sunlight were replaced with tendrils of dark clouds billowing like smoke into every crevice. The forest began to dance and sway in a hurricane-like wind that ripped through the trees and nearly knocked Merlin and Arthur off their feet. The noise of the wind was unlike anything Merlin had ever heard, and the teens covered their ears to block out the sound while crouching as low to the ground as possible.

Squinting against the debris flying around him, Merlin tried to discover the source of the violent storm. A bright light flashed throughout the entire sky, temporarily blinding him. In the darkness of the moment, the whipping and howl of the wind ceased. All was still and quiet and suddenly quite warm. Merlin blinked several times, trying to regain his sight, barely able to make out Arthur sprawled on the ground beside him. He appeared stunned but otherwise unharmed.

As their surroundings came into focus, the magician rubbed his eyes and shook his head in confusion. Instead of finding themselves in the wild, green forest, Merlin was perplexed to discover they were amid a barren wilderness. Few trees or plants dotted the landscape within his view. Yellow rocky sand stretched around him in all directions. Though everything else was different, the stone that had served as the resting place of the kingly sword looked remarkably the same in every respect, but one—Excalibur was gone.

"What happened?" Arthur asked, pressing his hand against his head and rising to a seated position. Looking around, he squinted at the harsh sunlight reflecting off the desert sand, then jumped to his feet. "Where are we? Merlin, what did you do?"

Merlin stood and circled the rock, hoping to see the sword, but it was nowhere to be found. A knot formed in the pit of his stomach. When he was younger, he had messed up spells before, but he'd never experienced a failure like this. Then again, he had never tried to use magic of such magnitude. "I don't know. I just cast a little spell to help you get the sword out. Something must have gone wrong."

"That, my friend, is the understatement of the year! Fix this. Send us back where we belong."

Merlin nodded. "Of course. All I need to do is say the reverse of the spell. That should make everything right again," though the young magician doubted things would be that simple. Pushing up his sleeves and taking a long, deep breath, he closed his eyes and uttered the reverse of the spell he had used moments before in the forest. The incantation complete, the young magician tensed for another gripping storm, but none came. Merlin opened one eye and peeked at his surroundings. Still sand. With another deep breath, he tried the spell again. The results were the same.

"Merlin!" Arthur whined. "Get us out of here, wherever here is!"

"I'm trying, but the spell isn't working."

"Then try a different spell."

Nodding, Merlin closed his eyes and let another incantation spill from his lips. The words came easily, skilled in his craft as he was, but no matter which spell or combination of spells he used, nothing happened. Frustrated, he sat down on the sand and hung his head between his knees. "I don't know what else to do. I've tried everything I know." He felt hot tears on his face and quickly wiped them away before Arthur saw them and accused him of being a baby. . .again!

Arthur plopped down on the ground beside Merlin, showering him with specks of sand. "Okay, there has to be an explanation for what's happened. Let's think this through. I'm sure we'll come up with an answer." Arthur wiped the sweat from his forehead. "In the meantime, how about you make yourself useful? Why don't you use your magic and conjure us up some water? It's hot and dry out here."

Merlin smiled. "Now that I can do." Holding out his hand, palm upward, the young magician whispered, "Aquae."

Nothing.

"Aquae," he said again, louder and more forcefully.

Once again, nothing happened. Merlin thrust his upturned hand toward the sky and cried, "Imber," attempting to cause a rainstorm, but his words had no effect.

"Don't tell me you've forgotten the spell." Arthur quipped.

"Worse," the young magician answered, turning to his friend in horror. "I think I've lost my magic."

A NOTE FROM THE AUTHOR

D EAR READER,

As you've embarked on this journey through the origins of Excalibur, you've explored the realms of myth and history, uncovering both the mysteries of legend and the truths woven into our world's tapestry.

Just as Excalibur has its roots in the depths of history, so does the salvation offered through Jesus Christ. While this story is fictional, it reminds us of a profound reality—the ultimate sacrifice Jesus made for our redemption.

In this short story, you've witnessed the power of a single sword to change the course of destiny. Similarly, the Bible tells of another life-altering choice—accepting Jesus as our Savior. It's a choice that offers eternal life, forgiveness, and a personal relationship with the Creator of the universe.

No matter where you are on your journey, I encourage you to explore this gift of salvation. It's not about religion; it's about a transformative relationship. It's about finding a refuge of faith and hope that can carry you through the most brutal storms, just as it did with the characters in this story.

Getting to know Jesus is as easy as ABC. First, admit you're a sinner in need of a Saviour. Second, believe in Jesus Christ, knowing that everything the Bible says about Him is accurate and that He is the only way to Heaven. Lastly, commit your life to Him, surrendering everything to His control. Salvation is about turning away from sin with all its pride and selfishness and turning to Jesus, who is full of love, compassion, and selflessness. It involves turning from death to life. Won't you choose Jesus today?

Please get in touch with me if you have questions or need any guidance. I'm here to help in any way I can.

Thank you for joining me on this adventure. May it inspire you to explore the most incredible story ever told—the story of God's love and redeeming sacrifice. John 3:16 says, "For God so loved the world, that he gave his only begotten Son, that whosoever believeth in him should not perish, but have everlasting life."

With warmest regards,
Renae Edwards

About the Author

Renae Edwards is a Christian fantasy author who lives in Wales and loves all things medieval. Her passion for writing started at a young age and she has pursued it ever since. Renae's stories are filled with adventure, magic, and faith. She loves to create worlds that are both familiar and fantastical, where readers can escape reality and discover something new. Through her work, Renae hopes to inspire others to use their God-given gifts and share their stories with the world. To learn more about Renae and her books, visit her website, RenaeEdwards.com or connect with her on TikTok and YouTube. She is always happy to chat with readers and fellow writers!

Printed in Poland
by Amazon Fulfillment
Poland Sp. z o.o., Wrocław

27174868R00057